Are You a Boy
or a Girl?

Kids spend a lot of time debating with each other over what makes a boy a boy and a girl a girl. It's a time of choices. It's a time of creating themselves. It could be a time for blending and embracing the many ways they express themselves, but is too often a time of narrowing the possibilities of who they can be. *Are You a Boy or a Girl?* enters into this conversation and opens it up. It is the story of a child thinking through who she is, a child learning through her mother's love how to be both strong and soft.

Karleen Pendleton Jiménez

Green Dragon Press
Toronto

Green Dragon Press
2267 Lake Shore Blvd. West, #1009
Toronto, ON M8V 3X2

Tel: 416-251-6366
Fax: 416-251-6365

Photographs and credits:

Cover and Page 1	**Karleen Pendleton Jiménez**
Page 3	**Dolls:** Hilary Cook
Page 4	**Carter Cook and Maya Condé-Kalmijn:** Hilary Cook
Page 5	**Karleen:** David Pendleton
	James Pendleton and David Pendleton
Page 6	**Karleen**
	Elaine Dee Jiménez McCann and David McCann
Page 7	**Karleen at various ages**
Page 8	**Karleen and Amy the dog**
Page 13	**Elaine Dee Jiménez McCann**
Page 14	(Top) **Adonica Huggins, Shahnaz Stri, Richard Pendleton**
	(Bottom) **Hilary Cook:** Heather Cook, **Shahnaz Stri**
Page 15	**Karleen:** Hilary Cook

Illustrations:	**Karleen Pendleton Jiménez**
Design:	Shadowcraft Imaging Group

ISBN 1-896781-14-4

Are You a Boy or a Girl?

There once was a girl who didn't like girl things,
no make up or dresses or dolls.
And the people who didn't know
that people are different
couldn't and wouldn't understand.

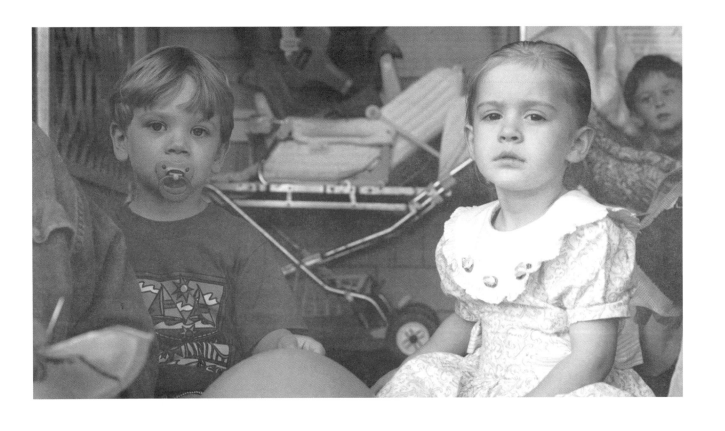

When she got her hair cut short
Sally in the sunflower dress asked,
"Are you a boy or a girl?"

And she whispered back,
"I'm a girl."

When she bought an airplane at the toy store
Berto in the blue baseball cap teased,
"Are you a boy or a girl?"

And she answered back,
"I'm a girl."

When she played basketball
Dionne in the dangly earrings taunted,
"Are you a boy or a girl?"

And she yelled back,
"I'm a girl!"

But nobody would believe her.
"You don't look like a girl
and you don't act like a girl
so there's no way you could be one."

This made the girl very sad.
She never thought about acting
like a girl or a boy,
she just did what she liked to do.

**Basketball and soccer and math and
playing her trumpet and eating cookies & cream
ice-cream.**

9

She didn't have time to think about it.
But someone would always ask,
"Are you a boy or a girl?"
And they never asked nice.
And sometimes they would laugh.
And the girl was so tired that she wanted to cry.
She grabbed her ball and ran.

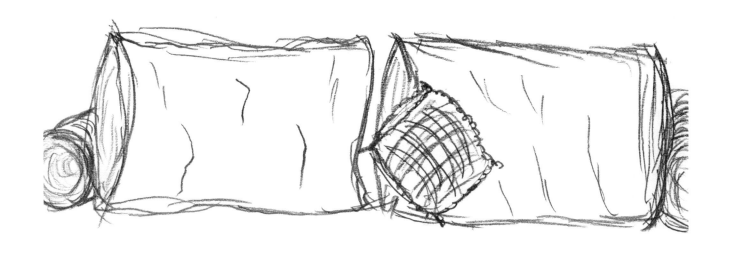

When she got home,
her mama saw her and was scared.
"Honey, what's wrong?" she asked
in long soft words that felt like pillows.

The girl jumped into her arms.
"Mama, every day they want to know
if I'm a boy or a girl
and they look at me like I'm a rat
or some hairy animal
and they point and make jokes."

Her mama took a deep breath and said,
"You'll never be a girl like other girls
and you'll never want to.
Right now it's hard
because too many people don't know about
girls like you.

But ever since there were girls and boys, there have been girls who like to do boy things and boys who like to do girl things.

14

And when you know that
and you're all grown up,
you'll know that you can do anything
you want to.
And that's the best way to live."

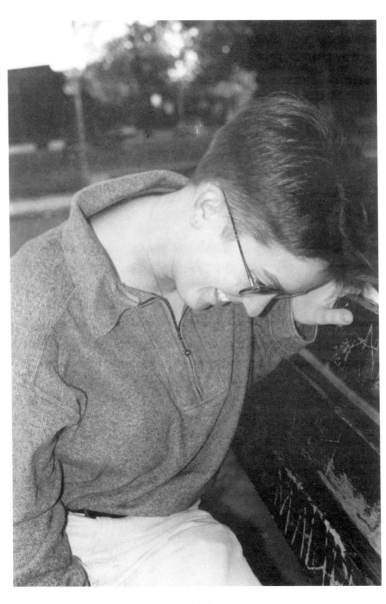

She looked at her daughter's wet brown eyes
and asked,
"Do you believe me?"

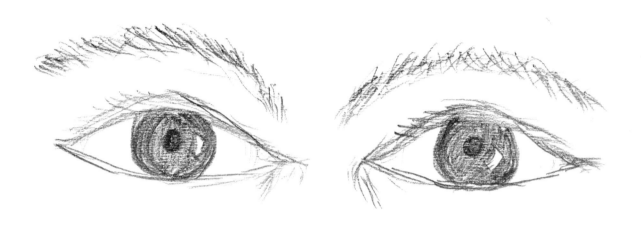

And she felt soft and safe curled into her
mama's big body
that smelled like yellow flowers and chocolates
and she believed her.